HAZEL ALLAN

WWW.STRIDENTPUBLISHING.CO.UK

Published by
Strident Publishing Ltd
22 Strathwhillan Drive
The Orchard, Hairmyres
East Kilbride G75 8GT

Tel: +44 (0)1355 220588
info@stridentpublishing.co.uk
breemccready@googlemail.com
www.stridentpublishing.co.uk

A catalogue record for this book is available from the British Library.

ISBN 1-905537-11-2 (10-digit)
and 978-1-905537-11-2 (13-digit)

Printed by Thomson Litho, East Kilbride, Scotland

1.
The Limerick Competition

Bree's heart sank faster than a brick in a swimming pool as Mrs Matlow eagerly informed the class about an impending limerick competition. Everyone had to take a partner and write a short verse about them using a festive theme. They would then have to read it out in front of everyone in the class – and their families – at the Christmas party on the second last day of term at Ramthorpe School.

To make it what Mrs Matlow called 'fair and exciting', their names were written on strips of paper and popped inside one of her jolly sunhats. The terribly thin and incurably clumsy woman, with shoulder-length ringlets and too many teeth to fit her mouth, danced and spun around the room like a spring lamb, stopping in front of each pupil so they could choose a name.

There was little point in Bree hoping that she would magically detect her best friend Sandy Greenfield's name in the neatly folded confetti at the bottom, for she was *convinced* which name she would see when she unfolded hers.

'Well, Bree?' Mrs Matlow shrieked excitedly. 'Put us out of our misery!'

There had been many, many moments in Bree's life when she had felt like vanishing in a puff of smoke and this was just another of them. Every single person in the class was staring directly at her and the room had become absolutely still. Her face started to sizzle with embarrassment and the more she tried to control it, the worse it got. The moisture in her mouth suddenly evaporated, making it impossible to speak. Eventually her pathetic voice left her lips and punctured the excruciating silence.

'It's Alice,' she said, with more than a hint of apology.

The stillness that filled the classroom was shattered by an abrupt tumult of laughter and sarcastic cheering.

'Lucky me,' sneered Alice Renshaw, rolling her eyes to the ceiling.

Perpetua Andulus, Alice's friend and protector, commiserated with a brawny arm around Alice's shoulder and fired an icy glare at Bree. Perpetua was a tall, muscular girl with oddly elongated limbs. She bulldozed all of the boys on the rugby field and could launch the javelin further than any of the gym teachers. She was not remotely popular in school but her brute strength was combined with a very short fuse, so everyone chose to stay on the right side of her temper.

Bree stared gloomily at the floor, hoping

it would open up and swallow her whole.

Alice was the prettiest, most popular girl at Ramthorpe. Secretly Bree *longed* to look like Alice and lay awake most nights wishing that when she looked in the mirror the next morning she would be surprised by her new flawless complexion and long shiny hair. Of course, it never happened.

By contrast, if Alice wanted to be anything like Bree she had a strange way of showing it. She snubbed Bree at every opportunity and only lowered herself to speak to her for two reasons: to make fun of her; and to get her help with homework, because Bree was the cleverest in the class. Alice had a nickname for Bree: Greedy McCready. But then it didn't help that even the teachers referred to Bree as 'slightly podgy'.

Oblivious to Bree's utter despair Mrs Matlow punched the air enthusiastically. 'Super Dooper!'

As she spun off, Bree kept her focus firmly on a piece of fluff woven into the wiry classroom carpet. She could scarcely believe her bad luck sometimes.

Once the last two pairings for the competition had been confirmed, Mrs Matlow clapped to get the attention of her class, who were now chatting animatedly.

'I shall look forward very much to hearing everybody's limericks at the Christmas party in a couple of weeks time.'

Bree sighed despondently and scrunched up her sliver of paper until her hand went numb.

Still, at least she had two weeks' reprieve.

However, those fourteen days flew past and suddenly the Christmas party was upon her. Ramthorpe School's gym hall throbbed with the sounds of music and laughter. Mrs Matlow danced round the pupils in her class, oblivious to the giggles at her unique moves. A string of silver tinsel wrapped around her neck complemented the flashing Santa Claus earrings which swung a blur of red and white as she jived.

Bree cupped her chin in her hands and tried her best to ignore the feeling of dread swelling inside her stomach like an over-inflated balloon.

'She might not to be *too* nasty,' shrugged Sandy, pushing his glasses up his nose, 'seeing as it's Christmas and everything.'

For as long as Bree could remember, Sandy's thick-rimmed glasses had always been far too big for him. They were forever slipping down, no matter how he tried to adapt them to fit his face, employing everything from a plaster to a lump of Plasticine.

Bree appreciated Sandy's optimism but knew he was as worried as she was about what Alice had in store for her. They slouched dismally, like two miserable bookends.

'Whatever happens,' he added, 'I'll be right there beside you.'

Bree knew she and Sandy were kindred spirits, two leaves caught up in the same breeze. She loved that she only had to look at him to feel that everything would turn out okay in the end.

And today Sandy was certainly doing his best to keep up her spirits, but nothing could assure her that the party would have a happy ending.

'I'll just be glad when it's over,' she said with an insipid smile and patted his knee gratefully. Mrs Matlow was flittering about on the stage. She fumbled with the music system, searching for the correct button to end the incessant singing about it being 'Christmas Every Day'. After a few seconds of frantic jabbing it ceased and as she was about to speak there was an excruciating screech which resonated around the wooden floored gym. Everyone stopped in their tracks and covered their ears. Half of the parents at the back of the hall grimaced and the other half exchanged understanding looks, relieved that it was not them up there having to grapple with confusing modern equipment.

The horrendous racket died down and was followed by a dull amplified thud as she tapped the microphone.

'Testing 1-2-3!'

A couple of parents gave the thumbs-up and Mrs Matlow flicked one end of the tinsel boa over her shoulder.

'Gosh golly!' she gushed, her hand fanned out over her chest, 'I feel like a popstar!'

There was a rush of encouraging laughter from the adults but everyone else cringed and groaned. As usual Mrs Matlow was blissfully unaware. She took a deep breath and smoothed down her flowery skirt.

'Now we come to the part of the evening we've all been waiting for,' she began a little more seriously. 'Would everyone please be seated so that we may begin The Limerick Competition.'

Bree and Sandy sat next to one another in the third row. Perpetua Andulus plonked her bulk in front of them and Alice joined her a few seconds later, wafting a sheet of paper in front of their faces. Despite craning his neck Sandy could not catch what was written on it but he *knew* it was the limerick about Bree. She nudged him in the ribs and he gave up trying to peer over Alice's shoulder. Bree chewed down hard on her thumbnail and tried to ignore the butterflies in her stomach. There was an atmosphere of nervous excitement, with pupils bobbing up and down, trying to grab the attention of family members who waved encouragingly from the back. Mrs Matlow called for silence and an expectant hush settled over the audience.

'I'm *very* excited to see everyone here today, and glad that so many friends and family could join us for our last Christmas party before my class embark upon their Senior School years.'

A round of enthusiastic clapping started at the back of the hall and, like a wave over their heads, worked its way right up to the stage. Mrs Matlow seemed overjoyed with the response.

'Thank you, thank you everyone,' she gushed breathlessly, curtsying and tossing her curly hair over her shoulder.

'Oh, for heaven's sake,' said Alice Renshaw rolling her eyes again. 'Anyone would think the woman had won an Oscar.'

Some of the class giggled as she folded her arms and pretended to yawn. Icy dread flushed Bree's soul as she realised that Alice was in full nasty mode.

'Could everybody kindly put their hands together for our first limerick,' instructed Mrs Matlow in her sing-song voice. 'Read by – em – now let me see...'

She shuffled some sheets of paper in front of her, juggling the microphone in one hand and her glasses, which hung from a chain round her neck, with the other.

'Ah, yes – *Miss Bree McCready!*'

A wave of grudging applause trickled its way up to the stage.

'Good luck,' encouraged Sandy, patting her on the back.

'I'll need it,' she replied, glancing over to Alice and Perpetua, who were staring at her, sneers pasted across their faces.

Mrs Matlow handed her the microphone and flashed one of her horsey smiles. Bree tried in vain to smile back but she was sure it must have looked more like a painful grimace to everyone watching. Looking out across the hall, she caught sight of her mother offering her unspoken encouragement and support.

There was an expectant hush. With every nerve and muscle in her body Bree fought to keep calm. She held the microphone in her sweaty palm, cleared her throat and looked at the audience.

'I've written my limerick about Alice Renshaw,' she muttered, looking at Sandy for assurance. Her voice sounded weak and unfamiliar as it travelled through the amplifier and ricocheted off the wall at the back of the gym.

Sandy winked at her from behind his

oversized glasses and for a brief moment she felt oddly calm. But then she glanced over at Alice, who was already shaking her head and whispering in Perpetua's ear. Bree swallowed hard.

'H-here goes,' she stammered, holding up her paper and hoping that no one would notice how it trembled in her hand.

'There was a young lady called Alice,
Who lived in a glorious palace.
When Christmas arrived,
She was never deprived,
Making all of her friends very jealous.'

The hall filled with a chorus of applause and cheers. For the first time that afternoon she allowed herself to smile. At the back of the hall her mother was doing her best not to jump up and down, but her fists were clenched in triumph and pride radiated from her pretty face, lighting the shadows at the back.

Even Alice Renshaw seemed satisfied with Bree's efforts and smiled smugly, lapping up the attention from the audience. When Bree got back to her seat, Sandy patted her on the shoulder.

'That was brilliant!' he said, pushing his glasses up his nose again.

'Not bad...' sniffed Alice, looking down her nose at Bree.

Bree smiled at the unexpected compliment and was almost on the verge of thanking her when Alice turned away and muttered to Perpetua. She felt the cold sting of hurt as she heard:

'For a fat cow!'

Alice and Perpetua collapsed in a fit of giggles and Bree felt her face redden.

'Just ignore them,' Sandy said protectively, shooting a look of disdain in the direction of the pair.

'That's easy for *you* to say,' whispered Bree, tears of embarrassment welling in her eyes. 'But she's up next.'

Having been the target of Alice's venom for so long she dared not even imagine the spiteful words that would be said in front of her classmates and her mother. As Alice strutted towards the stage Bree sank down low in her seat and braced herself for the worst.

'Ladies and Gentlemen, boys and girls,' announced Mrs Matlow. 'Please give a warm welcome to Bree's partner, Miss Alice Renshaw!'

The audience showed their appreciation with a bout of hearty clapping and Alice tossed her long, glossy hair over her shoulder.

'Get on with it,' muttered Sandy, yawning pointedly.

Perpetua threw him a vicious look from over her broad shoulder. Bree held her breath again, her stomach juddering as Alice unfolded the sheet of pink paper. She lifted the microphone to her mouth.

'There once was a poor lump named Bree,
Who plonked down on old Santa's knees.
When his chair legs gave way,
All he could say,
Was 'Next time, don't eat as much cheese!'

Perpetua roared with laughter. Alice folded the paper neatly, whispered, 'Thank you ladies and gentlemen,' into the microphone and smiled sweetly down at Bree.

There was a mortified silence from the back rows, followed by a spatter of uncertain applause. Bree was sure her blush was lighting up the entire hall. Some of the class turned in their seats to stare at her, laughing and pointing.

Perpetua's deep laugh shook the air, her shoulders rising and falling. Bree shrunk down further in her chair to avoid the hundreds of eyes that were now peering at her. The hall was now silent apart from a few giggles from her classmates. She bit her lip and willed herself not to cry. Alice Renshaw had returned to her seat and was leaning back, smiling conceitedly. When she flicked her long hair over her shoulders the ends brushed Bree's face, adding injury to insult.

Bree was overcome with relief when Mrs Matlow called up the next pupils, who read out their limericks to rapturous applause. Everything else was a blur. She could not even turn around to look at her mother. Her cheeks felt singed long after the last limerick had been read out and she tried to avoid looking either Alice or Perpetua in the eye. They occasionally glanced back at her and smirked.

After a short while Mrs Matlow went off to the side and re-appeared clutching a long rectangular parcel.

'Ladies and Gentlemen, after careful consideration I have chosen a winner for today's limerick competition…'

She left a suspenseful pause. Alice Renshaw grinned and prepared to stand up.

'Please congratulate *Miss Bree McCready!*'

Alice's lip-glossed mouth dropped open.

'It's a fix!' gasped Perpetua.

Bree could hardly believe her ears. She had never won anything in her life!

'Nice one,' laughed Sandy.

The audience clapped and cheered, not least Madeleine McCready. This time, when Bree walked up to the stage, she was smiling. 'Well done, my dear,' Mrs Matlow said as she placed her hand firmly on Bree's shoulder. 'You are a *very* deserving winner. I hope you are proud of yourself.'

'Well, that would be a first,' said Bree.

For a split second Bree thought that her teacher might actually cry. However, she thrust out the gaudily wrapped parcel. She was only vaguely aware of the applause as she clutched it in her trembling hands. She looked down at the red and gold wrapping and happiness hummed warmly inside her as she imagined ripping open the paper. She wanted to delay the moment for as long as possible, convinced that nothing would ever match this feeling, the weight of the parcel in her hands and the delicious thrill of anticipation. The applause continued as Bree walked back to her seat. Mrs Matlow had to shout into the microphone to be heard.

'There will now be a break for cookies and egg nog!'

She indicated a rickety old table disguised with a festive tablecloth, piled high with homemade Christmas cookies and mince pies. A murmuring buzz ran through the crowd and seats began to scrape.

There was a steady drizzle of background conversation as Bree carefully unpicked the wrapping. There seemed to be rather a lot of it and not much else. For a brief moment she thought this might be another joke at her expense. Was everybody about to burst out laughing as they watched the realisation dawn on her face that there was no prize after all? With increasingly desperate fingers she continued to unpeel layer after layer only to reveal nothing inside. As she tore at what looked like the final layer of thin cerise tissue, hope turned to despair. How would she cope with even *more* humiliation? Then something fell out, landing lightly on her lap. It was a gold locket on a chain. She quickly picked it up. It was one half of a heart. It was pretty but the serrated edge gave her the same hollow feeling she felt when she saw a paddling pool in the rain or a single, soggy glove stuck on a park railing.

Somewhere out there was another piece of heart which belonged with this one.

She let the locket dangle and swing, watching as little fragments of light reflected on its surface. It was then that she noticed the tiny inscription – six words stacked on top of one another:

LOOK

ON

SHELF

FOR

BOOK

SEVEN

Sandy had noticed the inscription too. He peered over the top of his glasses and squinted to read the words. Suddenly aware that Alice was also staring at the dangling locket, Bree dropped it into the palm of her hand. Alice did her best to look unimpressed.

'Cheap piece of tin,' she derided, her voice full of spite. 'I'm glad I didn't win if *that* was the prize. A pathetic prize for a pathetic girl.'

Bree took no notice. She looked down at the gold half-heart locket and thought it was the most beautiful thing she had ever seen.

When Bree was absolutely sure that Alice was out of earshot, she swung the locket in front of Sandy's face and lowered her voice to a whisper that only they could hear.

'What do you think it means?' she asked.

He strained short-sightedly, trying to read the inscription on the spinning locket, and twisted his mouth thoughtfully.

'Mmm. Sounds like an instruction. My guess would be to head for the school library,' he suggested.

'Let's go *right now,*' she exclaimed, shooting up out of her seat. 'Everyone's going home now and Thursday is Mrs Oxter's half day, so we'll be able to have a look around without anyone bothering us.'

She grabbed his arm and practically dragged him out of the hall.

Only one person noticed Bree and Sandy leaving by the side door. An ancient lady bent into the shape of a question mark. She sat alone with a serene smile on her wizened face and a twinkle in her one good eye as the other guests munched on mince pies and discussed late night shopping. None of them recognised her, but they had still smiled politely when they brushed past her to reach their seats. Despite her frailty she certainly stood out from the crowd, with her flowing white dress and moon-white hair. Beneath the wrinkles it was easy to tell that this crumpled, decrepit woman had once been very beautiful. She smiled contentedly as she watched Bree and Sandy sneak away with the locket, then let out a satisfied sigh, confident that everything was going to plan.

Thank you for supporting Bree, Sandy and Honey to this point in their adventure.

This is only the start. Things get even more exciting – and dangerous – after this.

If you are up for the adventure of a lifetime, buy or order your copy of *Bree McCready and the Half-Heart Locket* today. Available from all good bookshops, RRP £6.99.

And keep up with Bree McCready news at www.stridentpublishing.co.uk.

DarkIsle
ISBN 978-1-905537-05-1 (hardback, RRP £12.99)
ISBN 978-1-905537-04-4 (paperback, RRP £6.99)

When two strangers help Morag escape a life of drudgery she has no idea that joining them on their mission will take her into a world more dangerous than the one she is leaving behind.

An ancient stone that protects a mysterious homeland has been stolen by renegades intent on harnessing its powers. The only guide to its whereabouts is a dragon, turned to stone thirty years ago.

Morag's journey is perilous, with dark forces already afoot to stop her. Along the way are clues to the disappearance of Morag's own parents, urging her onwards to fulfil a destiny that seems inextricably linked to her own…

www.darkislethebook.co.uk

The Comet's Child
ISBN 978-1-905537-12-9 (paperback, RRP £7.99)

For as long as anyone can remember there have been rumours about the return of a chosen one. When Fin discovers the prophecies point to him he is scared, at first. He resolves to learn the truth about his origins and uncover the secrets surrounding his birth; only then can he embrace his true destiny.

The journey ahead is exciting and full of danger, but others must stop him before he learns the truth…

Lee and the Consul Mutants
ISBN 978-1-905537-01-3 (paperback, RRP £6.99)

It's not every day that a part of your body explodes, but Lee's appendix does exactly that, landing him in hospital.

Soon after his operation, Lee is shocked to discover that evil Consul Mutants are trying to take over the world. Worse still, the hospital he is stuck in contains the portal they are using to invade Earth.

Other kids might quake in their boots at this news, but not Lee. He's determined to save the world and comes up with a cunning plan to stop the aliens.

This is the story of a young boy battling against intergalactic odds for the sake of humankind. Lee's only weapon is his intelligence…which is a pity.

Lee Goes For Gold
ISBN 978-1-905537-00-6 (paperback, RRP £6.99)

Meeting his dad's multimillionaire boss inspires Lee to come up with a get-rich-quick scheme of his own.

But not everyone is keen for Lee to succeed. Local shopkeeper Panface certainly isn't, and it seems that he has sneaky spies on the case, trying to ruin Lee's plans.

Will Lee get the better of his rivals? Or will he spend the whole time daydreaming about how many houses he'll own and how many butlers he'll have?

Lee will need to rely on his common sense and financial genius if he's to succeed in business... so it could be a struggle.

Lee's Holiday Showdown
ISBN 978-1-9055374-02-0 (paperback, RRP £6.99)

Nothing is ever straightforward when Lee is around. Not even a summer holiday in Spain.

It ought to be a case of lazing by the pool, but Lee is soon spying on dodgy men in shiny suits and sunglasses, battling with a family that seems intent on ruining everyone's holiday, and haranguing horrendous holiday reps.

With so much going on, how will Lee ever get a tan?